The Delaware People

by Allison Lassieur

Consultants:

Jim Rementer
Project Director,
Lenape Language Project
The Delaware Tribe of Indians

Mark Peters
Chief/Historian
Munsee-Delaware Nation

Darryl Stonefish
Moraviantown Delaware

Bridgestone Books
an imprint of Capstone Press
Mankato, Minnesota

Bridgestone Books are published by Capstone Press
151 Good Counsel Drive, P.O. Box 669, Mankato, Minnesota 56002
http://www.capstone-press.com

Library of Congress Cataloging-in-Publication Data
Lassieur, Allison.
    The Delaware people / by Allison Lassieur.
      p. cm.—(Native peoples)
    Includes bibliographical references and index.
    Summary: An overview of the past and present lives of the Delaware (also known as
Lenape) Indians, including their history, homes, food, clothing, family life, customs,
religion, and government.
    ISBN 0-7368-1104-4
    1. Delaware Indians—History—Juvenile literature. 2. Delaware Indians—Social life
and customs—Juvenile literature. [1. Delaware Indians. 2. Indians of North America—
Middle Atlantic States.] I. Title. II. Series.
E99.D2 L39 2002
974'.004973—dc21

                                          2001003814

Editorial Credits
Tom Adamson, editor; Karen Risch, product planning editor; Timothy Halldin, cover
    and interior layout designer; Heidi Meyer, production designer and interior illustrator;
    Alta Schaffer, photo researcher

Photo Credits
Bettmann/Corbis, 14
Bob Krist/Corbis, 8
David M. Oestreicher, cover, 10
Francis G. Mayer/Corbis, 6
Photo by Jim Rementer, 12, 16, 18, 20

1 2 3 4 5 6 07 06 05 04 03 02

Table of Contents

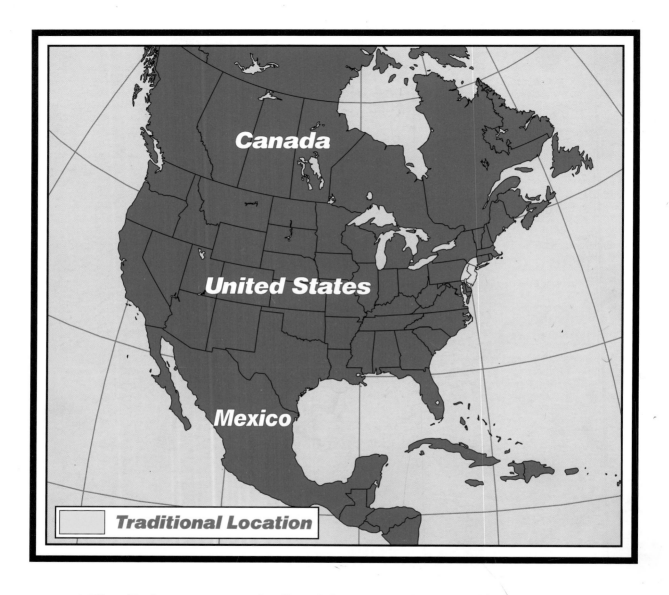

Canada

United States

Mexico

Traditional Location

The Delaware people lived in areas known today as New Jersey, New York, Pennsylvania, and northern Delaware. Today, most Delaware people live in Oklahoma and in Ontario, Canada.

Fast Facts

The Delaware people once lived in the northeastern United States. Today, there are separate groups of Delaware. Three groups live in Ontario, Canada. Two groups live in Oklahoma. But all Delaware have a common history. These facts tell about their history.

Homes: Long ago, the Delaware lived in different kinds of houses. In winter, some families lived in large longhouses. In summer, families built temporary homes that were small and round.

Food: The Delaware were farmers and hunters. They grew crops such as corn, squash, and beans. They gathered wild plants, nuts, and berries. The Delaware also hunted deer, elk, black bear, turkey, and buffalo.

Clothing: The Delaware wore clothes made of animal skins. After European explorers came to North America, the Delaware began wearing clothes made from cloth.

Language: The Delaware language is an Algonquian language. American Indians who lived in eastern North America spoke Algonquian languages.

The Walking Purchase

In 1737, a settler named Thomas Penn tricked the Delaware. The Delaware agreed to give Penn as much land as one person could walk in a day and a half. Penn found the fastest runners. He hired people to clear a path. The runners ran twice as far as the Delaware had thought they would. They had to give up a great deal of land.

Delaware History

Long ago, the Delaware lived in the northeastern United States. Most Delaware lived in small villages. People came together for celebrations during the year.

Europeans began coming to Delaware lands in the early 1600s. At first, the Delaware and the white settlers got along. Settlers taught the Delaware how to build log cabins and to raise livestock. The Delaware taught them how to grow corn and catch fish.

More white settlers came. They took land away from the Delaware. The Delaware started hunting game so they would have furs to trade with the settlers. Slowly, the Delaware began to rely on the settlers for some food and goods.

The settlers forced the tribe to move west. Some Delaware moved to Ohio. Others settled in western Pennsylvania. Three groups moved to Ontario, Canada. Most other Delaware moved to Oklahoma.

The European settlers and the Delaware got along at first. But later, the Europeans took the Delaware people's land away.

Delaware Groups

Long ago, the Delaware were divided into three different groups. The Minisink, Unami, and Unalactigo each spoke a different dialect, or form, of the Delaware language.

Minisink means "people of the stony country." They lived at the headwaters of the Delaware River. Unami means "people down the river." They lived in what is now northern New Jersey. Unalactigo means "people near the ocean." This group lived along the sea coast.

The Delaware People

The Delaware call themselves Lenape. Lenape means "original people." "Delaware" is not an American Indian word.

In 1610, a European explorer named Samuel Argall came to North America. He explored what is now Delaware and New Jersey. He also explored a river in this area. He named the river after an English nobleman named Thomas West, the Third Lord de la Warr. Settlers who came to America began calling the area "Delaware." They also used the name for the tribes that lived there.

Years ago, many other tribes respected the Delaware. They believed that the Delaware were the original tribe of all Algonquian-speaking people. Other tribes sometimes asked the Delaware to settle arguments. Today, many tribes still respect the Delaware in this way. They sometimes call the Delaware people "Our Grandfathers."

The Delaware people lived near the Delaware River.

Homes, Food, and Clothing

Long ago, some Delaware lived in longhouses. Some longhouses were up to 60 feet (18 meters) long. Delaware men pushed saplings into soft ground. They bent the tops of these young trees. They then tied the tops together to make a rounded roof. They made the walls out of tree bark.

The Delaware grew corn, squash, and beans. During summer, women gathered mushrooms, berries, and cattail roots. Men hunted and fished. They made lifelike decoys to attract ducks and other wild birds. They then killed the birds with bows and arrows. Delaware who lived near the sea caught scallops, clams, oysters, and crabs.

Before Europeans arrived, the Delaware made their clothing from animal skins. Men wore breechcloths in the summer. Women wore skirts. During winter, everyone wore leggings and moccasins. Most people also had coats made of beaver, bear, or raccoon fur.

The Delaware also built small, round houses called wigwams. They lived in wigwams during summer.

The Delaware Family

Long ago, the Delaware were divided into clans. A clan is a group of related families. Three main groups of clans used an animal for the symbol for their group. The animals were the wolf, turkey, and turtle.

A man and a woman had to be from two different clans to get married. When a Delaware couple got married, they moved into the wife's clan longhouse. Children belonged to the mother's clan. Their mother's brothers taught the children stories about their culture.

The clan system is not used much anymore. But some people still know to which clan they belong. Today, Delaware families live like most families in North America. The adults go to work and the children go to school. Grandparents or cousins may live with a family.

Many Delaware wear traditional clothing for ceremonies.

Manhattan Island

A famous story tells about how the Delaware sold Manhattan Island to Dutch settlers. In the story, the settlers gave the Delaware some beads and other goods. In return, the settlers took the whole island. The island later became part of New York City. The story makes the Delaware seem foolish for selling the island for such a small price.

Most Delaware think that this story is not true. Long ago, the Delaware did not believe that anyone could "own" land. Different groups had certain areas where they hunted and fished. But they did not own that land.

The Delaware probably did make a trade with a group of settlers. The Delaware thought they were giving the settlers permission to use the land for a little while. They believed that the Dutch were giving them gifts for this permission. Instead, the settlers thought they had "bought" the land. They kept the island for themselves.

Dutch settlers thought they had bought Manhattan Island for a few beads and other goods.

During the Big House ceremony, the Delaware prayed to Kishelemukong. They gave thanks for the fall harvest and asked for good crops for the coming year.

Delaware Religion

The Delaware believed that the world was created by Kishelemukong. This name means "He Who Creates Us by His Thoughts."

The Delaware believed the universe was divided into 12 levels. Earth was at the bottom level. Kishelemukong lived on the top level. Spirits called manituwak lived on the other levels. The Delaware believed that a person had to pray 12 times before the prayer would reach Kishelemukong. They also believed that it could take years for a person's spirit to reach Kishelemukong after death.

Long ago, the Delaware held a worship ceremony each fall. It took place at the Xingwikaon. This word means Big House. Services were held each night. Families camped near the Big House.

Today, many Delaware believe in Christianity. Christianity follows the teachings of Jesus. Some Delaware still tell the stories from their traditional religion. The stories remind them of their history.

Delaware Government

Years ago, the Delaware lived in many different small groups. Each group had its own chief and elders. These respected people made the decisions for the group.

Today, the Delaware are still divided into groups. Each group has its own system of government. The Delaware Tribe of Indians in Oklahoma has a seven-member Tribal Council. The tribe elects members of this council. Each person can serve on the council for four years.

The Munsee-Delaware Nation and Moraviantown Delaware in Canada have a different government system. They are each governed by a council made up of one chief and several council members. There is one council member per 100 people. The chiefs oversee the daily activities of their nation. The councils make decisions about business and other issues of their nation. Council members are elected every two years.

The Tribal Council of the Delaware Tribe of Indians meets in this building in Bartlesville, Oklahoma.

Why the Turtle Clan Is Best

The Delaware like to brag about their clan animal. They make jokes about the other two clan animals. One story tells why the Turtle Clan is the best.

One day, the three clan animals had an argument about who was best. As they argued, they came to a big river. The three animals saw food on the other side.

"I can get to the food," Turkey bragged. "So can I," argued Turtle. Wolf howled and ran up and down the riverbank. He was angry that he could not swim across the river.

Turkey took a running start and flew up above the water. But he got tired and fell into the water. He got back to shore where he started.

Turtle laughed at Wolf and Turkey. He stepped into the water. Turtle slowly crawled across the bottom of the river. He reached the other side and got the food. That is why the animals decided that the Turtle is the best, the Turkey next, and the Wolf last.

The Delaware tell stories to remember their traditional culture.

Hands On: Make Leaf Designs

Long ago, leaf designs were important to the Delaware. They used these designs to decorate their clothing and other objects. You can decorate paper with leaf designs.

What You Need

A few sheets of unlined paper
Leaves of different shapes and sizes
Pencil
Markers, paint, or crayons

What You Do

1. Collect leaves. They can be any kind of leaf. Try to find leaves that are different sizes.
2. Place the leaves along the edges of the unlined paper and trace around them. Use the same leaf pattern more than once, or try many different leaves for a different look.
3. Use the markers, paint, or crayons to color the leaf shapes. The Delaware liked bright colors such as red, blue, yellow, and green.
4. You also can draw pictures of animals, food, longhouses, or wigwams inside the leaf designs.

Words to Know

breechcloth (BREECH-kloth)—a waist covering made of cloth or animal skin

council (KOUN-suhl)—a group of leaders

decoy (DEE-koi)—a carved model of a bird used to attract real birds

Lenape (leh-NAH-pay)—the name the Delaware call themselves; the word means "original people."

livestock (LIVE-stok)—animals raised on a farm or ranch such as horses, sheep, and cows

manituwak (man-eh-TOO-wok)—spirits who live on different levels of the universe

religion (ri-LIJ-uhn)—spiritual beliefs that people follow

tradition (truh-DISH-uhn)—a custom, idea, or belief that is passed on to younger people by older relatives

Read More

Kraft, Herbert C. *The Lenape or Delaware Indians*. South Orange, N.J.: Seton Hall University Museum, 1996.

Sita, Lisa. *Indians of the Northeast: Traditions, History, Legends, and Life.* Native Americans. Milwaukee: Gareth Stevens, 2000.

Wilker, Josh. *The Lenape Indians.* The Junior Library of American Indians. New York: Chelsea Juniors, 1994.

Useful Addresses

Delaware Tribal Headquarters
220 NW Virginia
Bartlesville, OK 74003

Moraviantown Delaware
RR #3
Thamesville, ON N0P 2K0
Canada

Munsee-Delaware Nation
RR #1
Muncey, ON N0L 1Y0
Canada

Internet Sites

Delaware Tribe of Indians
http://www.delawaretribeofindians.nsn.us
Keepers of a Lost Culture
http://www.lihistory.com/2/hs208a.htm

Index